THE HEY DIDDLE DIDDLE PICTURE BOOK

BY

RANDOLPH CALDECOTT

CONTAINING

THE MILKMAID
HEY DIDDLE DIDDLE, AND BABY BUNTING
A FROG HE WOULD A-WOOING GO
THE FOX JUMPS OVER THE PARSON'S GATE

LONDON
FREDERICK WARNE AND CO, Ltd.
AND NEW YORK

Printed in Great Britain

THE MILK-MAID.

The MILKMAID.

An Old Song exhibited & explained in many designs by R. Caldecott.

— A LADY said to her Son — a poor young SQUIRE:
"You must seek a Wife with a Fortune!"

"WHERE are you going, my Pretty Maid?"
"I'm going a-milking, Sir," she said

"Shall I go with you, my Pretty Maid?"
"Oh yes, if you please, kind Sir," she said.

"What is your Father, my Pretty Maid?"

"My Father's a Farmer, Sir," she said.

"Shall I marry you, my Pretty Maid?"
"Oh thank you, kindly, Sir," she said.

"But what is your fortune, my pretty Maid?"

"My face is my fortune, Sir," she said.

"Then I can't marry you, my Pretty Maid!"
"Nobody asked you, Sir!" she said.

"Nobody asked you, Sir!" she said.

"Sir!" she said.

"Nobody asked you, Sir!" she said.

HEY DIDDLE DIDDLE

Hey, diddle, diddle,

The Cat

and the Fiddle,

The Cow jumped over the Moon,

The little Dog laughed

to see such fun,

And the Dish ran away with the Spoon.

BABY BUNTING.

Bye, Baby Bunting!

Father's

gone

a-hunting,

Gone to fetch

a Rabbit-skin

To wrap the Baby Bunting in.

A FROG HE WOULD
A-WOOING GO

A Frog he would a-wooing go,

    Heigho, says Rowley!

Whether his Mother would let him or no.

    With a rowley-powley, gammon and spinach.

    Heigho, says Anthony Rowley!

So off he set with his opera-hat,

  Heigho, says ROWLEY!

And on his way he met with a Rat.

  With a rowley-powley, gammon and spinach,

  Heigho, says ANTHONY ROWLEY!

4

"Pray, Mr. Rat, will you go with me,"
Heigho, says Rowley!
"Pretty Miss Mousey for to see?"
With a rowley-powley, gammon and spinach,
Heigho, says Anthony Rowley!

5

Now they soon arrived at Mousey's Hall,

Heigho, says ROWLEY!

And gave a loud knock, and gave a loud call.

With a rowley-powley, gammon and spinach,

Heigho, says ANTHONY ROWLEY!

7

"Pray, Miss Mousey, are you within?"

     Heigho, says Rowley!

"Oh, yes, kind Sirs, I'm sitting to spin."

With a rowley-powley, gammon and spinach,
Heigho, says ANTHONY ROWLEY!

"Pray, Miss Mouse, will you give us some beer?"

Heigho, says Rowley!

"For Froggy and I are fond of good cheer."

With a rowley-powley, gammon and spinach,

Heigho says, ANTHONY ROWLEY!

"Pray, Mr. FROG, will you give us a song?"

Heigho, says ROWLEY!

"But let it be something that's not very long."

With a rowley-powley, gammon and spinach,

Heigho, says ANTHONY ROWLEY!

"Indeed, Miss Mouse," replied Mr Frog,

   Heigho, says Rowley!

"A cold has made me as hoarse as a Hog."

   With a rowley-powley, gammon and spinach,

   Heigho, says Anthony Rowley!

"Since you have caught cold," Miss Mousey said,

Heigho, says Rowley!

"I'll sing you a song that I have just made."

With a rowley-powley, gammon and spinach,

Heigho, says Anthony Rowley!

But while they were all thus a merry-making,

   Heigho, says Rowley!

A Cat and her Kittens came tumbling in.

   With a rowley-powley, gammon and spinach,

   Heigho, says Anthony Rowley!

The Cat she seized the Rat by the crown;

Heigho, says ROWLEY!

The Kittens they pulled the little Mouse down.

With a rowley-powley, gammon and spinach,

Heigho, says ANTHONY ROWLEY!

This put Mr. Frog in a terrible fright;
        Heigho, says Rowley!
He took up his hat, and he wished them good night.
        With a rowley-powley, gammon and spinach,
        Heigho, says Anthony Rowley!

But as Froggy was crossing a silvery brook,

Heigho, says ROWLEY!

A lily-white Duck came and gobbled him up.

With a rowley-powley, gammon and spinach,

Heigho, says ANTHONY ROWLEY!

So there was an end of one, two, and three,
     Heigho, says Rowley!
The Rat, the Mouse, and the little Frog-gee!
     With a rowley-powley, gammon and spinach,
     Heigho, says Anthony Rowley!

THE FOX JUMPS OVER
THE PARSON'S GATE

THE Huntsman blows his horn in tne morn,

When folks goes hunting, oh!

When folks goes hunting, oh!

When folks goes hunting, oh!

The Huntsman blows his horn in the morn,

When folks goes hunting, oh!

The Fox jumps over the PARSON'S gate,
And the Hounds all after him go,
And the Hounds all after him go,
And the Hounds all after him go.

But all my fancy dwells on NANCY,
So I'll cry, TALLY-HO!
So I'll cry, TALLY-HO!

Now the PARSON had a pair to wed
    As the Hounds came full in view;
He tossed his surplice over his head,
    And bid them all adieu!

But all my fancy dwelt on NANCY,
    So he cried, TALLY-HO!
    So he cried, TALLY-HO!

Oh! never despise the soldier-lad
Though his station be but low,
Though his station be but low,
Though his station be but low.

But all my fancy dwells on NANCY,
So I'll cry, TALLY-HO!

16

Then pass around the can, my boys,

For we must homewards go,

For we must homewards go,

For we must homewards go.

And if you ask me of this song

The reason for to shew,

I don't exactly know—ow—ow

I don't exactly know

But all my fancy dwells on NANCY,

So I'll sing, TALLY-HO!

So I'll sing, TALLY-HO!

But all my fancy dwells on NANCY,

So I'll sing, TALLY-HO!

17